JACK AND THE BAKED BEANSTALK

BY *Colin Stimpson*

templar publishing
www.templarco.co.uk

Jack lived and worked in an old burger van with his mum and his dog Bella. Their sign read 'Fast Food', which was funny because the van's engine had broken down a long time ago and the van had stayed in the same place ever since, parked on the edge of the busy city.

Jack and his mum didn't really mind – they were proud of their little café. They kept the place clean, served tasty food and always had plenty of happy customers.

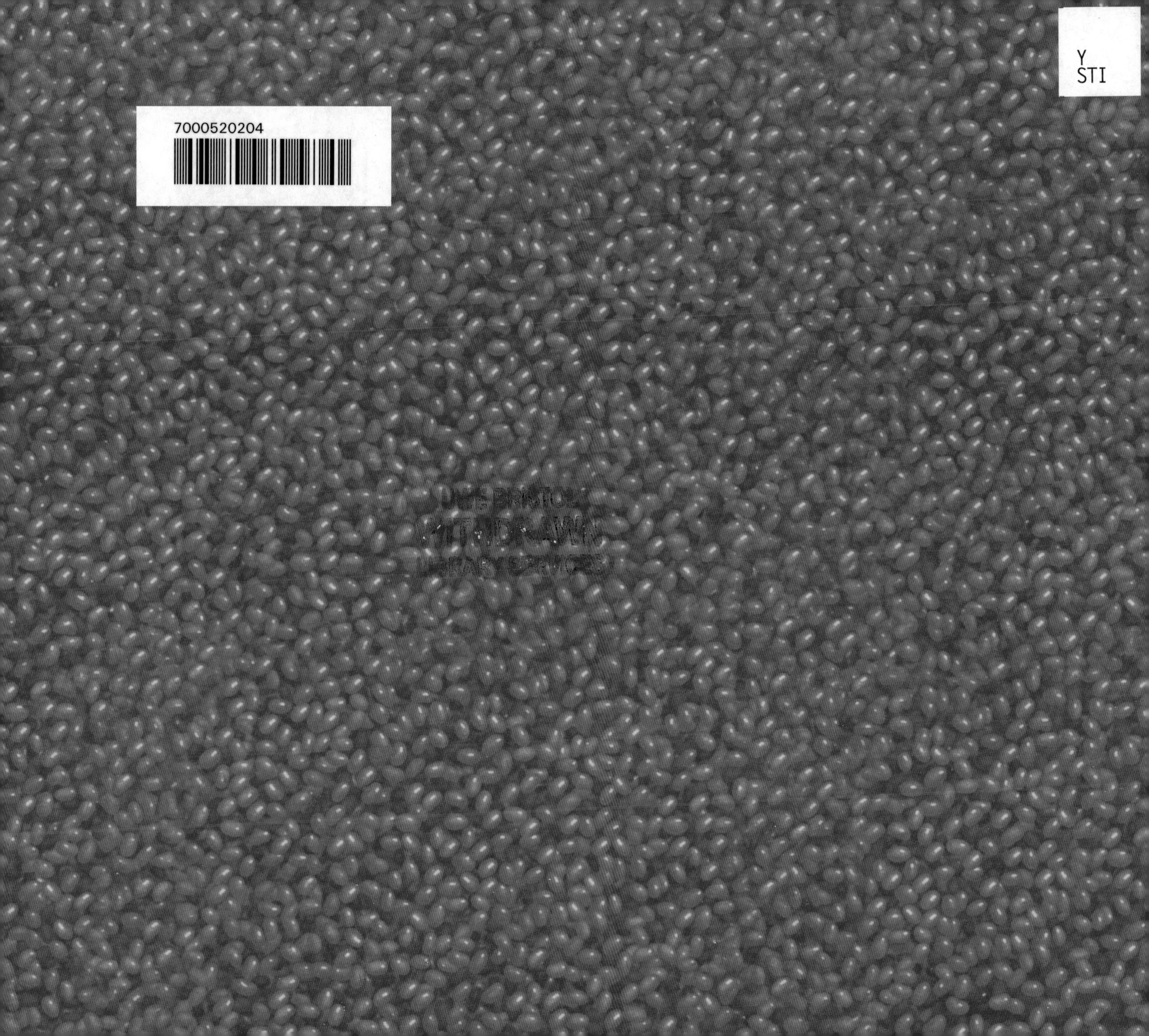

For my son, Jack — C.S.

A Templar Book

First published in the UK in 2012 by Templar Publishing,
an imprint of The Templar Company Limited,
The Granary, North Street, Dorking, Surrey, RH4 1DN, UK
www.templarco.co.uk

Copyright © 2012 by Colin Stimpson

First edition

All rights reserved

ISBN 978-1-84877-215-1

Designed by Mike Jolley
Edited by Libby Hamilton and A.J. Wood

Printed in China

One winter, the city council decided to build a huge flyover so that more people could get to work even faster. The old road where Jack's café stood was to be closed and soon construction began.

At first things didn't seem very different. Jack and his mum were kept busy feeding the builders eggs and sausages, burgers and chips, and lots and lots of cups of tea. When the flyover was finally complete, they were sad to wave goodbye to them.

All day long, traffic sped overhead as people hurried in and out of the city on the new flyover. Now they had such a fast way to travel, no one stopped to visit the old burger van any more. The new road had swept the customers away. Soon Jack and his mum were down to their last few pennies.

"Go to the shop and buy some milk and coffee beans, Jack. Everybody likes a good cup of coffee," said him mum, putting on a brave face.

On his way to the shops, Jack met an old man who asked him why he looked so sad. Jack explained about the flyover and his burger van.

"I think I can help you," said the old man thoughtfully. "Forget the coffee beans – these are magic baked beans. I wouldn't normally sell them, but you seem like a boy who would know their true worth."

Now, Jack had read enough fairy tales to know you don't turn down an offer like that. Also, baked beans were his favourite food in the whole world, so he couldn't resist tasting some magic ones. Thanking the man, Jack exchanged his last pennies for the beans and ran home.

"You did what?" shouted his mum, when Jack showed her the can of beans

"But Mum, they're magic baked beans. The old man promised," argued Jack, realising how silly he sounded.

Furious, his mum threw the can out of the window and sent Jack straight to bed without any supper.

Early the next morning, Jack woke up to find his room bathed in a curious green light. Strange branches twisted in through the window and at the end of each shoot dangled a silver can of baked beans.

"It's a magic baked beanstalk!" Jack whispered to Bella, trying not to wake his mum. "If I remember rightly there should be heaps of treasure at the top."

After hurriedly eating a breakfast of the best beans Jack had ever tasted, he crept outside.

"Are you ready Bella?" said Jack, grabbing hold of a long green tendril. "Mum will be worried when she notices we've gone, but if this really is a magic beanstalk, she'll forget about being cross when we bring her back some treasure!"

Up between the leaves they climbed, high into the sky. Finally, Jack and Bella reached the top, just above the clouds. The last branch wound its way to the steps of the biggest castle Jack had ever seen.

Squeezing under the front door, Jack found himself in an enormous room. Suddenly there was a bone-shaking clunk, then another and another, followed by the sound of someone singing:

"Fee-fi-fo-fummy –
I'm always counting money.
Be it silver or be it gold,
it'll make me happy,
or so I'm told."

Sure enough, Jack could see towers of golden coins stacked up in front of an enormous table and, behind it, an even more enormous giant.

"Uh-oh!" whispered Jack. "I'd forgotten about that bit of the story..."

But just as Jack and Bella turned to run, the giant spotted them.

A *huge* hand reached down and scooped Jack and Bella high up in the air before dropping them on his table. In front of them was the most enormous chicken Jack had ever seen.

"We have visitors," boomed the giant.

"So I see," squawked the chicken.

"And we know just what to do with visitors, don't we?" said the giant. "Now you STAY THERE – I'll be back in a jiffy." And with that the giant grabbed a handful of the chicken's eggs and marched off to his kitchen. Soon the sound of clattering pots and pans was making the table tremble.

"Is he going to eat us, Chicken?" squeaked Jack, shaking with fear.

"**Don't** be silly!" cackled the chicken. "He just wants to make you some lunch – he hasn't cooked for someone new in a long, long time."

As Jack watched, the giant switched on an enormous radio. Then, his foot tapping along to the sound of the music, he began to make the biggest omelette Jack had ever seen. While wonderful smells wafted into the room, the chicken told Jack about life in the castle.

"Every day, all day, the giant counts his money," she clucked. "He doesn't know what else to do with himself and it's hard for the radio – she's a magic one you know – she can only play at lunchtime, as the giant needs silence when he's counting."

Just then the giant appeared.

"Lunch is ready!" he cried cheerfully.

Over lunch Jack told the giant all about life at the bottom of the beanstalk and the giant told Jack about his money. Jack thought having such treasure was fantastic but the counting sounded a bit... well, boring.

"I do get pretty lonely up here," confessed the giant. "Would you consider staying? You could help me count and I could cook us tasty meals."

"Sorry," said Jack, "I just couldn't leave my mum. I should be getting back."

"Can I come with you?" sang a small voice. Jack and the giant turned to the radio in surprise. "I want to play songs all day long."

"And I've always wanted to stretch my wings," clucked the chicken.

The giant looked glum, but agreed that his friends deserved a change after all their years in the castle.

With a heavy heart, the giant walked them all to the top of the beanstalk.

"Are you sure you won't come with us?" asked Jack. "If this was the fairy tale, you'd be chasing us all the way down."

"I'd love to," said that giant sadly, "but, truth be told, I've always been a bit scared of heights and it looks a long way down that beanstalk. I'd better stay here and count my gold."

So Jack and Bella climbed onto the chicken's back and, clutching the radio, began the long journey back to the ground.

"Goodbye, goodbye," hollered the giant, waiving his handkerchief. "Do come again soon." But as he leaned out over the top of the beanstalk, trying to catch a last glimpse of his friends, there was suddenly a loud CRACK...

"*Snap!*" went the beanstalk, and down, down, down fell the giant. Crash, bang, wallop, right on top of the new flyover.

*C*ars skidded in all directions, but fortunately no one was hurt.

"Are you all right?" asked Jack, who had luckily reached the ground just in time.

"No," said the giant, as an enormous tear splashed onto the concrete below, then another and another. "Now the beanstalk's broken, I can't go home. And without my money to count, I've got nothing to do. Whatever will become of me?"

"It isn't that bad," said Jack thoughtfully. "At least you're with your friends and if you tried doing something you enjoy, you might find it more interesting than counting money."

And that is the story of how the Baked Beanstalk Café became the famous place it is today. It's much bigger than the old place, in almost every way.

If you're ever passing, I suggest you call in. You can say hello to the giant chicken or listen to the jumbo radio that plays fantastic music all day. The baked beans and eggs are always free and, to top it all, they have a very, very famous cook...

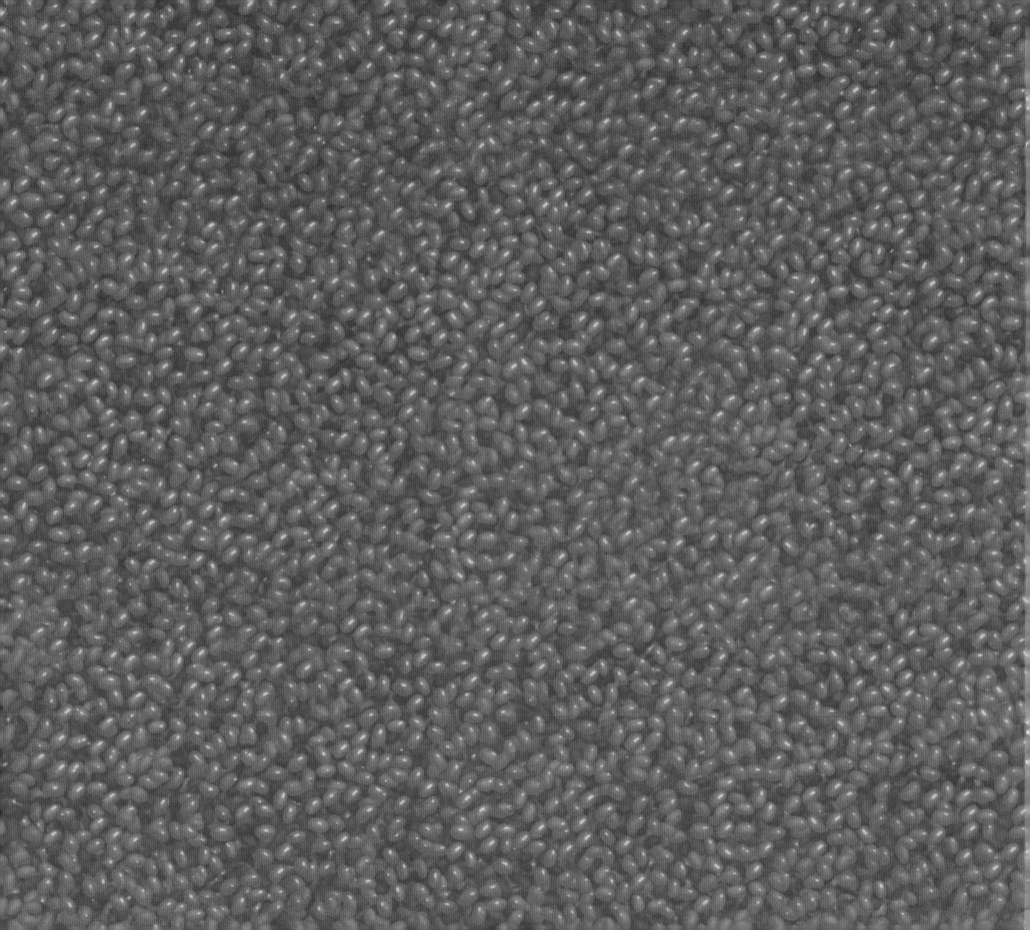